Nobody, Him and Me

For Chloe, with love – S.A.H.

For my father, with love – P.G.

First published in 2001 by Macmillan Children's Books
A division of Macmillan Publishers Limited,
20 New Wharf Road, London N1 9RR
Basingstoke and Oxford
Associated companies worldwide
www.panmacmillan.com

ISBN 0 333 97359 3 PB

A CIP catalogue record for this book is available from the British Library.

Printed in China

Nobody, Him and Me

SANDRA ANN HORN

Illustrated by PANTELIS GEORGIOU

MACMILLAN
CHILDREN'S BOOKS

Mother Mouse and her three baby mice lived in an old windmill. Mother Mouse crept out in the night and gathered up the spilt grain from the millstones. The miller never saw her slipping through the shadows. She was very quiet.

Mother Mouse was getting old and tired, and her eyes were not as sharp as they used to be. Over the years she'd had many children – so many that she'd run out of names for them.

One by one they grew up and went their own ways, until only the three little ones were left.

One day, the three little mice were playing tag.
Faster and faster round the table they ran, up over
the chairs – and CRASH!

"Whatever was that?" said the miller.

"Mice, most likely," said his wife.

"We'll have to get a cat."

"Look what you have done!" cried Mother Mouse.
"Now the miller knows we're here, we shall have no peace.
Who started that silly game?" There was no answer.

"I'm waiting," said cross Mother Mouse.

The three little mice all spoke at once:

"Nobody!"

"Him!"

"Me! Oops, no it wasn't!"

"Well, Nobody, Him and Me, you can *all* go to bed,
right now!" said Mother Mouse, and off they went.

Next morning, a box arrived
at the windmill.

There was something howling
and yowling inside. There was
something jumping and
bumping. Green eyes stared
and sharp claws scratched.

On the label was written:
Biter the Fighter.

"Oh," said Mother Mouse,
"this will be the end of us!"

Biter the Fighter prowled and scowled.
He showed his spiky teeth.

"I am the mighty Biter!" he roared down the mousehole.
"I always get my mouse."

Mother Mouse came over all faint and had to sit down.

When it was night, Mother Mouse peeped out.
The cat was sitting on the grain sacks close by.
His claws gleamed in the moonlight. He was asleep
with one eye open.

Mother Mouse quivered and quaked.

"Ooh, I daren't go out there!" she squeaked.

"But we're hungry, Mother!" cried the three little mice.

"It's no use! I'm frightened," she said, and put her
apron over her head.

"We'll go, Mother," said the three little mice.

They tiptoed out of the mousehole. Closer and closer to the sacks they crept. Nobody reached out a small, shaky paw towards the grain.

Biter sprang!

"Eeek!" said Me.

"Squeak!" said Him.

They dashed for home, dragging Nobody behind them. They tumbled head over paws into the mousehole, just as Biter landed. He glared in at them with one green eye and snarled, "I'll get you next time!"

"We'll just have to move away!"
sobbed Mother Mouse.

"Not us," said the three little mice,
when they got their breath back.
"We'll think of something,
Mother, don't worry."

They whispered together in the corner.

They drew arrows and circles in the dust.

"Right," they said, "here we go!"

They marched out of the mousehole.

Biter licked his lips when the three little mice appeared. Nobody, Him and Me began to run.

They ran round and round Biter. Two ran one way, one ran the other. Biter started to pounce, but he didn't know which way to jump. Faster and faster ran Nobody, Him and Me. Biter began to spin round in a circle.

"All change!" called Nobody, and they ran the other way.
Biter's feet got in a tangle and he fell over. He was dizzy.
He didn't feel very well.

The mice ran up the
wall and onto a beam.

"Come and get us!" they called.

They waggled their ears at him.

"I am Nobody the Cat Walloper!"

"I am Me the Mighty!"

"I am Him the Hero!"

"You can't catch us for toffee-nuts!"
they shouted.

Biter's head was still spinning,
but he just had to get those mice.

"Yoo-hoo, pussy-cat! Here we are!" they called. Nobody, Him
and Me were now on the very highest beam.

Biter scrambled up after them. He had almost made it when
he looked down – and remembered he was scared of heights . . .

In the morning, the miller and his wife called,
"Biter! Puss! Where are you?"

High above their heads they heard a faint, "Help!"

"How ever did you get up there?" said the miller.
He fetched a long ladder and brought the trembling
cat down.

"I was scared," mumbled Biter. "I was too high up."

"Why?" said the miller's wife.

"It was Him made me do it!" sobbed Biter.

"No, it jolly wasn't!" said the miller.
"I was in bed and snoring all night long."

"Aye," said the miller's wife.

"Nobody made me do it!" squeaked Biter.

"Eh?" said the miller's wife.

"It was Me!" yelled Biter. "Me teased me and
Me muddled me, so I chased Me up the roof."

"Wife," said the miller, "call the vet."

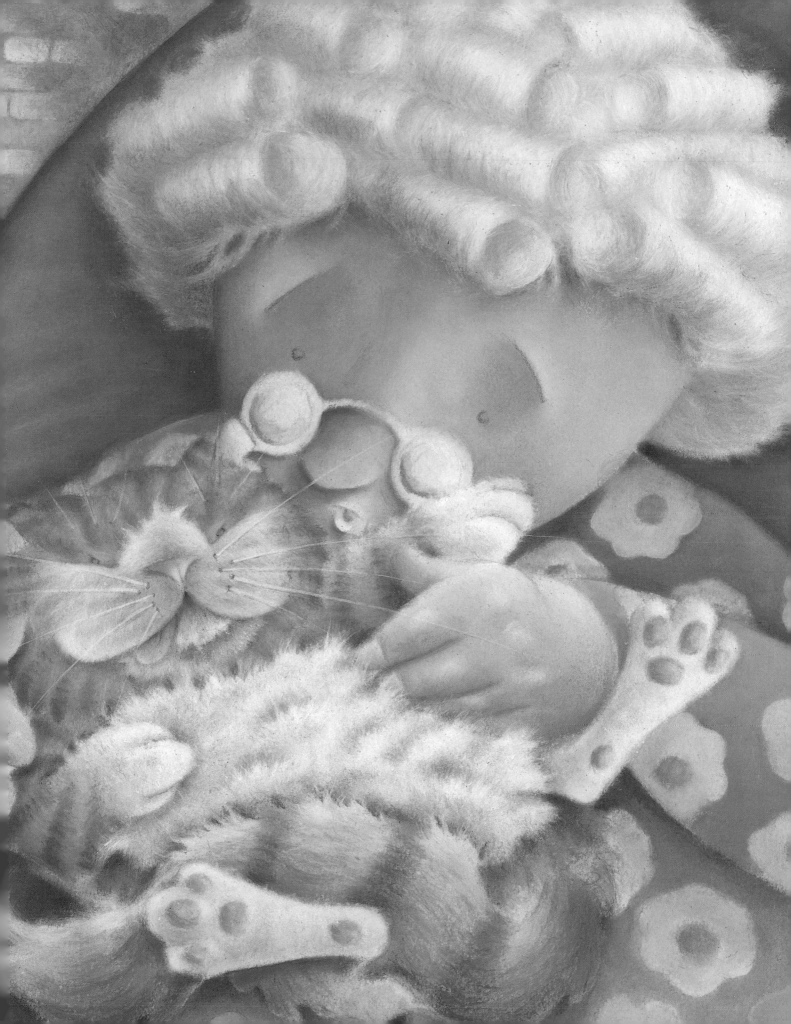

"There, there," said the vet. "Poor thing. He is too highly strung for mill work. It has turned his brain. I'll take him to Mrs Kindly's Rest Home for Distressed Cats."

"Are there any mice there?" asked Biter.

"I'm afraid not, old chap," said the vet.

"Thank goodness," sighed Biter.

He was carried away on a cushion.

Nobody, Him and Me still live in the windmill with Mother Mouse. She stays at home knitting stripy socks, and they creep out and gather up the spilt grain.

They are very, very quiet.

Mother Mouse and her children lived happily
in the old mill . . . until the day the miller bought a cat –
Biter the Fighter. But the mice are smarter than the miller
thinks and they soon hatch a cunning plan . . .

MACMILLAN

£4.99

ISBN 0-333-97359-3

90100

9 780333 973592

Usborne
PICTURE WORLD HISTORY
DINOSAURS